A GHOST^{IN} THE ATTIC

SUZAN REID

Illustrations by
SUSAN GARDOS

Scholastic Canada Ltd.

Canadian Cataloguing in Publication Data

Reid, Suzan
   A ghost in the attic

(Shooting Star)
ISBN 0-590-03867-2

I. Title.   II. Series.
PS8585.E607G46 1998   jC813'.54   C98-931029-9
PZ7.R44Gh 1998

76543   Printed in Canada   01234 / 0

Contents

This book is dedicated to my sisters: Karen (thanks for the laughter and the understanding), Cindy (thanks for the phone calls when I need them most) and Tracy (thanks for reminding me what I was like as a kid).
Also dedicated to my husband Dan (thanks for giving up the computer every now and then so I can write).

Chapter 1

A Face in the Window

"Come on, Matt, hurry up!" Jaime called as she ran up the school steps.

Matt stood at the bottom. "You're crazy," he said.

Jaime turned around as she pulled open the front door. "Matt, I saw what I saw. Let's go check it out."

"A ghost?" asked Matt. "You're telling me that you saw a ghost in the attic of the school?"

Matt shook his head and sat on the bottom step.

Jaime let the door close and ran down the steps to sit beside Matt.

"I saw it," she assured him. "I saw it with my own eyes."

Matt rolled his eyes. "What did it look like?" he asked.

"I don't know. It looked like . . . like . . . like a face in a window. Then it moved."

"So? Somebody's up in the attic and they looked out the window. It doesn't have to be a ghost, you know." Matt turned to face his best friend. "Your imagination is always working overtime. My mom says — "

"I know, I know," Jaime interrupted. "You don't have to tell me." It was her turn to roll her eyes.

"My mom has known you a long time," said Matt. "She knows you very well." It was true. Matt and Jaime had been friends since they were babies.

Jaime glanced toward the attic window. "It

wasn't just any face, Matt. It looked different. Maybe somebody is trapped up there."

"If somebody was trapped up there, or locked in, don't you think they would be banging on the window?" asked Matt as he bent over to tie his loose shoelace.

"You're right," answered Jaime. "It must be a ghost."

Matt sat up again. "Jaime! Think about it. If you were a ghost, would you hang around this school? There are a lot more interesting places to haunt than a school. Like a castle or some-place exciting." Matt slapped his forehead. "What am I saying? There is no ghost!"

"There is one. I saw it," Jaime said in exasperation. "And if it's hanging around in the school attic, I'll bet there's a secret up there!"

"Come on, Jaime," Matt sighed. "You thought there was a secret down in the basement too. Then you started thinking everyone was an alien!"

Jaime bit her lip, remembering how her

imagination got carried away on that one.

"Not everyone," she defended herself. "Anyway, this is different, Matt!"

"You always say that!" groaned Matt as he sunk his head into his hands.

"Come on," Jaime grabbed Matt's hand and pulled him up and along the path. They walked to the spot where she had seen something in the window. "Just wait," she said as she sat down on the grass. She took her glasses out of her pocket and put them on. "I want to be ready when it comes back."

Matt sat down beside her. "We should really just worry about making sure we get to class on time," he said. "The bell's already gone."

"Just a second," Jaime insisted as she stared at the window.

"Remember?" Matt reminded her. "We promised Mrs. Rupert that we would watch our behaviour. I don't want another deten- tion." Their teacher had kept them in after school a few days ago because they had caused a disruption.

Jaime continued to stare at the window. It remained empty. "Sorry, Matt," she said as she stood up and brushed off her jeans. "I guess it was my imagination. Maybe your mom is right."

"You should maybe get your glasses checked," joked Matt as he stood up.

"Very funny. At least I'm wearing them," said Jaime. She took one more look toward the attic window. "Matt . . . " she stammered, poking his arm.

"What?" asked Matt.

"Look!" she pointed toward the window.

"Jaime, for crying out loud . . . " Matt sighed as he looked up.

Way up in the window of the attic, a face appeared. It looked down at Matt and Jaime, then disappeared.

Jaime stepped back. "See?" she shouted. "See? I told you there was something up there!"

Matt stared at Jaime, then back at the window. "I may live to regret this," he said, "but . . . I saw something too."

"We've got to get up there!" said Jaime in excitement.

Slowly, Matt nodded his head.

Chapter 2

In the Staff Room

Matt and Jaime sprang through the front doors of the school and slipped past the office.

"Hurry up," Jaime said, "let's check it out before class starts."

"We don't have time, Jaime. Hold on, my shoelace is undone again," Matt said. He bent over to tie it up.

Mrs. Rupert almost fell over him as she stepped out of the staff room. Her coffee cup tottered and coffee lapped over the sides and onto the floor. Mrs. Rupert looked down.

"Matt Dias," she sighed.

Matt managed a weak smile. "Good morning, Mrs. Rupert."

Mrs. Rupert glanced up the hallway where Jaime was standing against the wall. "You're both going in the wrong direction this morning," she commented. "Grab some paper towels from the staff room, will you, Matt?"

Jaime sauntered back along the hallway. "Good morning, Mrs. Rupert," she said.

"Good morning to you, Miss Forrester. Where are you two off to?"

"We were looking for something," Jaime answered. Matt emerged from the staff room and Jaime grabbed a wad of the paper towels he was carrying.

"I've got to run to class," Mrs. Rupert said. "Do you two mind cleaning this up? It shouldn't take too long."

"We don't mind at all," said Jaime as she began wiping up the coffee spill.

"I'll see you in the classroom in a few minutes," said Mrs. Rupert. She started toward the classroom and then turned around. "You won't be long, right?"

Matt and Jaime looked up. "No, Mrs. Rupert. We'll be there in a few minutes," Jaime assured her.

"Good," said Mrs. Rupert as she turned around again. "See you then."

"It's almost as if she doesn't trust us," whispered Jaime as she finished cleaning up the spill.

"Would you?" asked Matt.

"What do you mean?"

"I mean, I think that she thinks we're kind of strange. We acted pretty strange in class the other day, when we thought she was an alien."

Jaime laughed. "Maybe she is!" Matt frowned at her. "Just kidding, Matt. Sheesh." She grabbed Matt's elbow before he stood up. "Do you think the attic is locked?" she asked.

Matt shrugged. "I don't know. I've never been up there before."

"I'll bet it's locked," Jaime said quickly, "but I'll bet Mrs. Rupert has a key."

"Why would Mrs. Rupert have a key?" asked Matt. He stood up and stepped toward the staff room.

"Teachers have keys for everything," Jaime answered. "Quick! You run up and see if it's locked. I'll put these in the garbage." She grabbed Matt's wad of paper towels.

"All right," sighed Matt. He ran toward the stairs.

Jaime tossed the paper towels into the staff room garbage bin and glanced around. On the far wall were rows and rows of pictures. Jaime stepped closer to the pictures and walked along, looking at each one.

"It's locked," panted Matt as he ran into the staff room.

"Thought so," said Jaime. "Hey, Matt, check this out."

Matt stepped closer and recognized one of the faces. "That's Mr. Douglas," he said.

"It must be all the principals of the school."

Jaime pushed her glasses further up her nose and moved back across the room.

"Look at this lady!" Matt said. "Check out her hairdo!"

"I think that's called a beehive," giggled Jaime.

"That's a good name for it. Look at this one. You should be thankful that you don't have to wear glasses like that!" Matt said.

"Pretty strange-looking," agreed Jaime.

"This must be the first principal," said Matt as he stood in front of the largest picture on the wall. "Stanley Fulton," he read.

"Stanley?"

"That's what it says. Stanley Fulton, 1914 to 1937."

Jaime leaned over Matt's shoulder to get a closer look. She stepped back in surprise.

"That's the face — " she gasped.

Matt turned around. "Jaime, what's wrong?" he asked.

Jaime's eyes were wide. "That's the face I saw in the attic window."

Matt turned slowly around to re-examine the picture. Stanley Fulton's face stared back at them.

"I can't believe I'm saying this, but you could be right," whispered Matt.

"Hey, cowpokes, you're late for class," announced Mr. Douglas as he stepped into the staff room. "Why are you two in here?"

Matt and Jaime spun around. "Oh, hi, Mr. Douglas," said Matt. "We were just cleaning up a mess in the hallway."

"Mrs. Rupert ran into Matt and spilled her coffee," Jaime added. "We just cleaned it up."

"Ah," said Mr. Douglas. He opened the fridge and pulled out a carton of juice. "Looking at the pictures, are you? Fulton Street School has had a lot of principals. Not a great picture of me," he said as he glanced at his photo. "Should have worn the other tie." He leaned closer to the picture and wiped the glass with his finger. "These things sure get dusty."

Jaime pointed to the picture of Stanley

Fulton. "Who's this guy?" she asked.

Mr. Douglas took a glass from the cupboard and poured himself some orange juice. "That's Stanley Fulton. He was the very first principal here. They named the street and the school after him."

"What was he like?" asked Jaime.

"Well, I don't rightly know too much about him," said Mr Douglas. "He was here a long while. Twenty years or more. I hear he was a real fanatic about dinosaurs."

"Fanatic? What do you mean?" asked Matt.

"I mean he was fascinated by them," answered Mr. Douglas. "He had pictures of dinosaurs all over his office. He read about them all the time. He kept track of all the newest discoveries."

"Oh," said Jaime as she nodded her head. "That's an interesting hobby."

"I suppose so." Mr. Douglas took a sip of his orange juice and swirled it around and around in his mouth. He took a long time to swallow it.

"What happened to him?" asked Jaime.

Mr. Douglas took another sip of orange juice. Again he swirled it around and around in his mouth before swallowing it. "Funny thing," he answered.

"Funny thing?" asked Jaime as her eyes began to grow wide. "You mean funny ha-ha or funny strange?"

"He never came back," Mr. Douglas answered.

Jaime looked at Matt. Matt shook his head, then closed his eyes. *Oh, no!* he thought.

"What do you mean he never came back, Mr. Douglas?" asked Jaime.

Mr. Douglas took another sip of orange juice. Jaime watched his cheeks swirling it around and around. Slowly he swallowed it.

"People say he was here on the last day of school, putting things away . . . "

"In the attic?" asked Jaime in anticipation.

Mr. Douglas frowned. "Yes, I guess he could have been up there. Don't rightly know for sure, mind you. Anyway, they say Stanley

Fulton was talking a lot about some 'rock springs.' After that day, no one around here ever saw Stanley Fulton again."

"Rock springs?" asked Matt. "What are they?"

"Hmmm . . . " Mr. Douglas thought, then shook his head. "I read something about it once, but I can't remember. Maybe Stanley Fulton was going a little — you know — kooky." He tilted his head. "Being a principal for that long might do strange things to a person!"

"Would Matt Dias and Jaime Forrester report to their classroom immediately," Mrs. Herron's voice interrupted over the speakers.

"The secretary's calling us," said Matt.

"Goodness!" exclaimed Mr. Douglas. "We've been chewing the fat here and I've kept you. Mrs. Rupert must wonder where you are." Mr. Douglas pulled a large ring of keys from his pocket. "I've got to go and open up the equipment room for Mr. Cavin. He's lost his keys again. Gallop along now, cowpokes!" he said.

"If only we could find Mr. Cavin's missing keys." Jaime said as they started down the hallway.

"The grade seven teacher? How would we find his keys?" asked Matt.

"I'm not sure. But somebody always finds them somewhere. He just puts them down and forgets where he put them. Remember when Jordan found them last month in the library?"

"Yeah, so?" Matt knew what Jaime was leading up to. He just wasn't sure he wanted to hear it.

"If we found them, we could open up the attic," said Jaime patiently. "We could find out what the secret is — why Stanley Fulton disappeared."

"If there is a secret," Matt reminded her.

"This is getting interesting," Jaime said as she opened the door to the classroom. Mrs. Rupert stopped reading *The Secret World of Og* and frowned at Matt and Jaime.

"Sorry we're late," apologized Jaime as she slid into her seat.

"Um-hmm," said Mrs. Rupert.

Matt pulled his novel out of his desk. "She's not going to let us leave the classroom for any reason today," he whispered to Jaime.

"Excuse me, Matt," said Mrs. Rupert. "Is there something you want to share with the class?"

Matt turned around to face his teacher. "No, Mrs. Rupert."

"Then you won't mind if I interrupt your conversation with Jaime. We'd like to get back to reading." Mrs. Rupert stood up. "In fact . . . " she began.

"Oh no," groaned Jaime as she watched Mrs. Rupert scan the classroom.

"Let's see . . . " Mrs. Rupert continued. "Let's have Jaime switch places with Cory."

"I knew that was coming," Jaime mumbled as she stood up. Matt picked up one side of Jaime's desk and helped her move it one row back and one over. Cory's desk slid into Jaime's old spot.

Mrs. Rupert opened up her novel. "You can save your visiting for lunch time," she said to Jaime.

Matt was in the middle of answering questions to Chapter Five when a wad of paper landed on his book. He glanced over at Jaime. She motioned for him to open it up and read it.

But Mrs. Rupert's hand was waiting. "This must be very important," she said. She scooped up the wad of paper and put it in her pocket. She glanced at Jaime, then Matt. "I'll see you two at lunch time."

"Lunch time?" asked Jaime.

Mrs. Rupert turned around and walked back to the front of the classroom.

"Yes, lunch time," she answered. "We'll all eat lunch together and get everything straightened out."

"Eat lunch together?" Jaime was horrified.

"Is that a problem?" asked Mrs. Rupert as

she began tapping her pencil on her desk.

Jaime looked at Matt. He shrugged. "No, Mrs. Rupert. It's not a problem," Jaime answered. "I've just never had lunch with a teacher before." Some students in the classroom giggled.

"Then it will be an interesting first experience for you," Mrs. Rupert answered. "Now, let's get back to work here. Let's put our novels away and get started on some math. Jessica, would you hand out the protractors?"

As Jessica began handing out supplies, Jaime sighed. "I hope lunch time never gets here," she groaned.

Chapter 3

Lunch with Mrs. Rupert

The lunch bell rang. The other students put their books away, got their lunches out of their backpacks and left the classroom. Matt and Jaime remained at their desks.

"You can go and get your lunches," said Mrs. Rupert as she pulled hers out of her briefcase.

"I'm on the hot lunch program," said Jaime. "I have to pick up my lunch in the lunch-room."

Mrs. Rupert frowned. "Okay, I'll go and get it for you. The two of you stay right here." She quickly left the classroom.

Jaime scrambled across the room and sat down in Cory's desk.

"What did the note say?" asked Matt.

"It said: 'Let's try passing notes. Don't get caught.' " answered Jaime.

"Too late for that," sighed Matt.

"Anyway, I've been thinking about this attic thing all morning," Jaime said.

"I knew you would. So? What have you come up with?" asked Matt.

"I can't figure it out. There was definitely something or somebody in that window. And it definitely looked like Stanley Fulton."

Matt nodded his head. "I know we saw something, Jaime. But really, how could it be Stanley Fulton?"

Jaime sighed. "Of course it's not Stanley Fulton," she said. "It's his ghost. Don't you know why ghosts haunt old houses and creepy places?"

Matt tilted his head. "No, why?"

Jaime grabbed his arms. "Because they have — " she glanced quickly around the classroom " — unfinished business," she whispered.

Matt leaned back. "They have what?"

"Unfinished business," Jaime continued. "I saw it on *Mysterious Happenings* once. There was a ghost in this family's house. The ghost roamed around moaning something about baseball. The family found an old baseball card hidden behind one of the walls. After that the ghost and the baseball card disappeared." Jaime took a deep breath. "It was freaky," she added.

"I see," said Matt as he slowly nodded his head. "So now you think there's a ghost roaming the attic of the school. You think this ghost is Stanley Fulton because he mysteriously disappeared. You think you need to figure out why he's haunting the school, and that will solve Stanley's problem and then he can go where all the happy ghosts go?"

"Something like that," replied Jaime.

"Do you know how ridiculous that sounds?" asked Matt.

"Here you go," said Mrs. Rupert as she entered the room with Jaime's lunch tray. She plunked the tray down on Jaime's desk and went to retrieve her lunch bag. Mrs. Rupert pulled up a chair beside Jaime's desk and opened her bag. "Now, let's talk about why you're here," she said.

"It looks like you have a tuna fish sandwich," Jaime said to Mrs. Rupert. "Tuna fish is good. Why, just the other day, I said to my mom, 'You just can't have enough tuna fish.'"

"Jaime . . . " started Mrs. Rupert.

"In fact," Jaime continued, "I think I could eat tuna fish every day. Could you eat tuna fish every day, Mrs. Rupert?"

"Jaime . . . " Mrs. Rupert said again.

"In fact, I'll bet I could even have tuna fish for breakfast. Have you ever had tuna fish for breakfast, Mrs. Rupert?" Jaime rambled on.

"Jaime!" snapped Mrs. Rupert. "We are not

here to discuss tuna fish. You're trying to change the subject. We are here to discuss this note. Come to think of it, I also need to know why you were so late for class this morning. It shouldn't have taken you that long to clean up the coffee spill. Let's start with this, though," she said as she pulled the note out of her pocket and placed it on the desk.

"Jaime? What do you have to say about it?" she asked.

Mrs. Rupert took a big bite out of her sandwich. Jaime blew on her soup. Matt opened his lunch bag. Mrs. Rupert waited. She swallowed her mouthful, sighed heavily and turned to face Matt. "Matt?" she asked. "Maybe you have something to say."

Matt opened his chocolate pudding. "Well ... " he began.

"Oh dear, dear," interrupted Mrs. Rupert. "You mustn't eat your pudding first. Where's your sandwich?"

Matt rummaged through his lunch bag and pulled out his sandwich. "Well," he continued, "we were passing that note and I know it's not right and we'll never do it again," he said.

"I see," said Mrs. Rupert. "Jaime, don't slurp your soup like that. It sounds horrible."

Jaime glanced up and managed to nod. "Sorry," she said. "And I'm sorry about the note too. It won't happen again."

"And why were you so late this morning?" asked Mrs. Rupert. "Matt, you are getting crumbs all over your shirt."

Matt wiped away the crumbs and swallowed his mouthful of sandwich. "We were talking to Mr. Douglas," he replied. "We were looking at all the pictures of the principals in the staff room and we just forgot about the time. Sorry we were late."

"Pictures of the principals? Yes, some of the stories there are very interesting," said Mrs. Rupert as she dabbed at her lips with a napkin.

"He was telling us about Stanley Fulton," said Jaime. "About how he disappeared."

"Yes, yes, what an interesting story. People

say that he just decided to . . . " Jaime and Matt leaned closer to Mrs. Rupert. Mrs. Rupert stopped. She shook her head.

"We are not here to talk about that," she said. "We are here to make sure that your behaviour improves. No more coming into class late, and no more notes. You two have been in your share of trouble lately, it seems." She looked at the two students. "I need to see some improvement or there will be more serious consequences. All right?" She waited.

Matt and Jaime nodded their heads.

"Good!" Mrs. Rupert said as she closed up her lunch bag. "Finish your lunches and then you can head outside for a while. Get some fresh air. I'll return your tray to the lunchroom."

"Thank you, Mrs. Rupert," said Jaime.

As soon as their teacher was gone, Jaime stuffed her apple into her pocket. Matt put his lunch bag into his backpack and stood up. "I think she was going to say something about Stanley Fulton," he said.

"I think so too!" exclaimed Jaime. "She obviously knows something about why he disappeared."

Jaime headed toward the door. Then she stopped. "Next week is spring break. We have only four days to find some keys and figure everything out!" She grabbed her friend's shirt-sleeve and pulled. "Come on, Matt. Let's see if we can get into the attic now. Maybe someone left it open!"

Chapter 4

Detention

Jaime and Matt raced up the attic stairs. Jaime jostled the doorknob. "Still locked," she sighed.

"Well, that's that, then. We'll have to try and find some keys," said Matt.

Jaime grabbed his elbow as he turned to walk back down the stairs. "Wait!" she cried. "Maybe we can open it another way."

"Like how?" Matt asked.

"I don't know, like in those spy movies. They use other things to open locked doors." Jaime answered.

"Like what?"

"I don't know. What have you got?"

Matt stood up and reached into his pockets. "I have a stick of gum."

"Quick! Let me have it!" Jaime reached for the gum and poked it through the keyhole.

"You're squishing it all up!" Matt cried.

Jaime handed it back to him. "It doesn't work anyway."

Matt looked at his mangled gum. "Thanks a lot," he said.

"What else have you got? A bobby pin? Those things work really good."

Matt rolled his eyes. "A bobby pin? Why would I have one of those? I don't exactly wear them in my hair, you know."

Jaime tapped on the door impatiently. "Anything else? Don't you have anything?" She stood up and rummaged through her own pockets. She grinned. "A paper clip!

From my book report!"

"Will it work?" asked Matt.

"I think it might," Jaime answered as she worked at unbending it. "Let's see," she said as she squatted down and began to jimmy the lock.

"Anything happening?" asked Matt.

"Not yet . . . " she answered.

"Here, let me work at it for a while," offered Matt.

Jaime handed him the paper clip. "Go ahead."

Matt peered through the keyhole and then stuck the paper clip into the hole. "What do you do? Just move it around?"

"Yeah, until it clicks." Jaime sat down on the step beside him. "You try it for a while and then give it back to me. I'll try again."

Jaime and Matt tried many times. Finally, a voice over the PA system interrupted them.

"Would Matt Dias and Jaime Forrester please report to their classroom."

Jaime gasped. "Is lunch over already?"

"I didn't hear the bell!" Matt exclaimed. He handed the paper clip to Jaime. "Man oh man, are we ever in trouble now."

"Come on, we'll try this again later," said Jaime as she stuffed the paper clip into her pocket. Jaime could see Mrs. Rupert as soon as she reached the bottom of the stairs.

"She's waiting for us," said Matt.

"She looks pretty mad," noticed Jaime.

"She doesn't look happy, that's for sure," agreed Matt.

"Late again?" asked Mrs. Rupert as she tapped her foot on the floor. "After what we discussed at lunch? What were you doing up there anyway? Come on, let's get going," she said abruptly as she began walking down the hallway.

"We're really sorry, Mrs. Rupert." Jaime caught up with her and began to explain. "We were so caught up in something that we lost track of time and . . . "

"Never mind." Mrs. Rupert frowned. "You can explain everything after school. We'll have to phone your parents, of course," she said as they walked into the classroom. "I warned you there would be consequences."

"Our parents?" asked Jaime.

"Yes, your parents," answered Mrs. Rupert. "We need to do something together, before the situation gets any worse. For now," she sighed, "let's just get through the afternoon."

The afternoon dragged on. When the bell finally rang, Jaime and Matt remained in their seats once again.

"I'm going to call your parents now," said Mrs. Rupert as she walked toward the front door of the classroom. "I'll be right back."

"My mom isn't going to be very happy about this," sighed Matt.

"Mine either," Jaime responded. "But maybe we've discovered something here. If we find out what happened to Stanley Fulton, everyone will understand. They might even have a parade or something for us, and everyone will laugh about how much trouble we got into!"

Matt raised his eyebrows, then shook his

head. "I really don't think that's going to happen. A parade in our honour?" He laughed aloud at the mere thought of it. "Can you imagine?"

"Hey, it could happen," Jaime insisted. "Anything's possible."

"Well, well . . . " came a voice from the doorway. "It's you two again."

Jaime looked up. "Hi, Mr. Turkle," she said sheepishly. Once, she had thought he was an alien. She and Matt had even followed him around the mall, trying to figure out what he was up to on Earth.

Mr. Turkle emptied the garbage into a large bin. He looked at Matt and Jaime and then shook his head. "Can't seem to stay out of trouble, can you?"

Matt shrugged. "We're having a bad day."

"I'd say so," Mr. Turkle said before he left the classroom.

"Maybe he could lead the band at our parade!" Matt exclaimed.

Jaime burst into laughter.

"Having a bit too much fun in detention," said Mrs. Rupert as she walked into the classroom. "I've managed to contact both of your parents. There will be action taken at home."

"No TV," said Matt.

"No telephone," said Jaime.

"At any rate," continued Mrs. Rupert, "we'll deal with you at school first. You'll complete some assigned work here until three-thirty. Then you will be on garbage detail until four o'clock."

"Garbage detail?" groaned Jaime.

"Cleaning up the schoolyard. There's quite a bit of garbage out there, and it will be your job to clean it all up. Mr. Douglas will supervise you outside."

"The whole schoolyard?" asked Jaime.

Mrs. Rupert frowned. "The whole school-yard," she answered. "In the meantime, here's some work for you to do," she said. She handed them some papers. "I'll be right at my desk if you need any help."

"We're going to be here a long time," Jaime whispered to Matt.

"Problem?" asked Mrs. Rupert.

"No," answered Jaime.

"If I'm not mistaken, Miss Forrester, I believe I moved your desk over there." Mrs. Rupert motioned with her pencil to where Jaime's desk was.

Jaime shrugged. "I guess I'm just used to sitting in this spot," she answered. She stood up and moved from Cory's seat into her own.

The clock ticked noisily on the wall behind Mrs. Rupert. Jaime glanced up every few minutes to check the time.

Finally Mrs. Rupert spoke. "Okay," she began as she laid two large garbage bags on her desk, "now it's time for you to pick up garbage." Matt and Jaime picked up the bags. "Do a good job," Mrs. Rupert said. "I look forward to improved behaviour tomorrow."

Jaime glanced at Matt before she answered. "We'll try," she said.

"You'll try very hard," Mrs. Rupert corrected her.

"Yes, Mrs. Rupert." Jaime nodded her head. "We'll try very hard."

Chapter 5

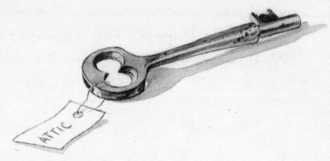

The Key

Mr. Douglas was waiting for them in front of the office. "Well, I'll be hornswoggled," he said. "Two new recruits for garbage detail. I don't believe you've ever done this before."

Jaime shook her head. "No, Mr. Douglas. We've seen other kids do it, though."

"All the litter on the fields and around the back fence," Mr. Douglas instructed. Jaime and Matt nodded. "Well, let's get a move on, cowpokes. Let's head 'em out!"

"Where should we start?" asked Matt.

"Clean up the front first, then move on to the back field," answered Mr. Douglas. He opened the front doors of the school and the two friends walked down the steps.

"Let's do this quickly," said Jaime. "Then maybe we'll have time to try the paper clip again in the keyhole."

"I think I've had enough excitement for one day," sighed Matt as he headed toward the monkey bars.

In a few minutes, they were done. "Is that good enough, Mr. Douglas?" Jaime asked as she looked around the front of the school. "I think we got everything."

Mr. Douglas nodded. "Looks pretty good," he agreed. "There's a garbage bin right over there," he said, pointing to a large garbage pail at the bottom of the stairs.

Matt nodded his head in agreement. "Can we do the back field now?" he asked.

"Back field? Oh, yes, the back field. Well,

you get started and I'll be right out," answered Mr. Douglas as he stepped into the school. Jaime and Matt rounded the corner and started picking up litter in the back field. Within a few minutes Mr. Douglas was standing on the steps waving his arms. "Jaime!" he called. "Your mother is on the phone and would like to talk to you!"

Jaime turned to look for Matt, who was over in the corner of the field by the back fence. She dropped her garbage bag. "I'm coming!" she answered.

Slowly she walked down the hallway toward Mr. Douglas's office. She could hear Mr. Douglas on the phone as she neared the office. " . . . fine idea. We'll get to the bottom of this," he said. Jaime winced. "Thank you for your call, Mrs. Forrester. Jaime's on her way to the phone now."

Jaime opened the door. Mr. Douglas held out the receiver so that she could take it. He motioned for her to sit down in his chair.

Jaime sat down and took the phone from

him. "Hi, Mom," she said as Mr. Douglas left the office and closed the door. "I know . . . I'm sorry . . . I'm just not having a very good day." Jaime began twirling the cord around her finger. "I know . . . but we didn't hear the bell!" She shifted in her chair and spun around to face another wall. "Okay, Mom. I promise."

She glanced at all of the objects on the wall. Her eyes widened. "What, Mom? Yes, I'm still here. Okay, okay. Yes, I know. I'll see you when I get home. Bye."

Jaime hung up the phone and quickly rose from the chair. On the wall was a large corkboard. Attached to the cork was a large number of keys. Jaime glanced toward the door, then went to the corkboard. She reached up to examine the keys. Each one had a coloured label on it.

"Library . . . storage space . . . janitor's room . . . these are all the spare keys!" she whispered. She glanced toward the door again and then quickly returned her attention to the board. "Art supply . . . science cupboard . . ."

She grinned as she turned over the next key and read the label. "Attic!"

Jaime heard a sound and turned to look at the door again. The doorknob was turning! She jumped, and the key fell off the corkboard and onto the floor. She scooped it up and tucked it in her pocket.

"All done?" asked Mr. Douglas.

"Yes, Mr. Douglas. I'm all done."

"I was chewing the fat with your mother, Miss Forrester," said Mr. Douglas. "I reckon you know she's a little worried about you."

"Yes, I suppose she is," answered Jaime as they started down the hallway.

"Come by my office tomorrow morning and we'll have a little chat, how about that?" suggested Mr. Douglas.

Jaime nodded. "Okay."

"Now, you'd better get that field finished."

Jaime bounded down the back steps and ran across the field to where Matt was. "Where have you been?" he demanded. "I thought maybe you'd gone home or something."

"My mom called to talk to Mr. Douglas," Jaime panted. "Then she wanted to talk to me."

"Well, come on, I'd like to get this finished."

Jaime dug into her pocket. "Look what I've got!" she exclaimed.

Matt dropped his garbage bag. "Where did you get that?" he asked. "Or do I want to know?"

"It was hanging on a wall in Mr. Douglas's office," Jaime answered.

Matt groaned and slapped his forehead. "You took a key from the principal's office?"

"Not took," Jaime corrected him. "Borrowed. We'll put it back."

"Without anyone noticing that it's missing?" asked Matt.

"There's a zillion keys, no one will notice," Jaime assured him.

Matt picked up his garbage bag. "No more today, please, Jaime. The attic can wait until tomorrow."

"I know," Jaime answered. "I have to go in and talk to Mr. Douglas in the morning, but we'll do it right after that!"

Chapter 6

In the Attic

The next morning, Jaime and Matt wheeled their bikes into the school parking lot.

"I was dying to phone you last night," said Jaime, "but Mom said no telephone for a week."

"No TV for me," Matt complained. "I missed all my favourite shows. It was awful."

They locked up their bikes and Jaime headed toward the school entrance.

"Where are you going?" Matt asked.

"Remember? I have to see Mr. Douglas," Jaime answered.

"Oh, yeah. I'll see you later, then." Matt waved. "Good luck."

Jaime entered the school. The door clanged behind her as she stepped into the empty hallway. *The school looks different when it's empty*, she thought. *Like I'm not supposed to be in it.*

"Ah, Miss Forrester!" Mr. Douglas stepped out of his office. "Glad you remembered to come!"

"Good morning, Mr. Douglas," Jaime said politely. "How are you today?"

"Dandy! I have someone here who would like to talk to you," he said as he ushered Jaime into his office. "This is Mr. Roberts. He's here to help you work out what's bothering you."

Jaime blinked. "Oh," she said. "Hi."

Mr. Roberts smiled. "Perhaps you've seen me around here before. I talk with a few of the kids at this school."

"I guess so," said Jaime.

"I'll leave you to it, then," said Mr. Douglas.

Jaime and Mr. Roberts talked for a while. He was a very nice man. He had spoken to Jaime's mom too. She had mentioned that Jaime seemed obsessed with aliens. Jaime assured Mr. Roberts that she wasn't thinking about aliens anymore.

Mr. Roberts smiled when the session was over. "I hope that was helpful, Jaime," he said. "If you need to talk any time, just let me know."

"Okay," Jaime answered as she closed the door.

Matt was waiting on the stairs. "How did it go?" he asked.

Jaime shrugged. "A guy named Mr. Roberts was there."

"What did he want?" asked Matt.

"I don't know. To talk about stuff," Jaime answered. She glanced at her watch. "We have twenty minutes before the bell! Come on! Let's check out the attic!" Jaime scurried around the corner and scrambled up the attic steps. Matt followed closely behind.

"Slow down, will you, Jaime?" he called.

"We don't have much time," Jaime called back. "Remember? We said we wouldn't be late for class again." She dug into her pocket and pulled out the key. "Are you ready?" she asked.

"Ready as I'll ever be," said Matt.

Jaime slid the large key into the keyhole and gently turned it. The door clicked open.

"Bingo!" whispered Jaime. Slowly, she turned the doorknob.

"For crying out loud, Jaime, would you hurry up?" Matt said.

"I don't want to frighten anyone who might be inside," whispered Jaime.

"For heaven's sake!" Matt said in exasperation. He grabbed for the doorknob and pushed the door.

The door swung in toward the darkened room. Its hinges creaked and moaned. Matt leaned inside and reached for the light switch.

"Why are you banging on the wall?" asked Jaime.

"I can't find the switch," Matt answered. He stepped through the doorway.

Jaime stepped in behind him. "Maybe it's on this side of the door," she suggested. She started to move down the wall, patting it as she went.

"Find it yet?" Matt asked.

"Nope. It's got to be on your side. Here, let me help you look." Jaime turned and stepped toward Matt. Then she let out a scream.

"A spider web! Get it off me!" Jaime shook her head violently. "It's in my hair!"

"Jaime! Jaime! Stand still!"

"I think the spider went down my back! It did!" Jaime began to dance around, shaking her head and her arms.

"Jaime!" Matt grabbed her wrist. "Stand still!"

Jaime slowly turned her head and looked back. "Is it on me?"

Matt was holding the end of a long string in

his hand. He looked up. "You didn't find a spider web, Jaime. You found the light switch." He pulled the cord, and a dim light came on.

Jaime stared around the room. Cupboards and shelves lined one wall. Trunks and boxes were piled up against another. "Look at all the stuff up here," she said in amazement.

"Yeah, there's obviously no room for a ghost," joked Matt.

Jaime stepped toward the window. "This is where the face was," she said as she placed her hand on the glass. "This is where the ghost was standing." She glanced down to the floor. "Right here."

Matt dusted off the labels on some of the boxes and trunks. "These have years written on them," he said.

Jaime came to look. "What do you think is inside them?" she asked.

"Don't know," answered Matt. "Here's one that says 1975." He lifted the lid off the box.

"What's inside?" asked Jaime.

"Here's a whole bunch of class pictures. Man, they look weird."

Jaime glanced over his shoulder. "Your sister wears stuff like that now! Look at those shoes. Zoe wears those all the time."

Matt burst out laughing. "You're right!" He placed the pictures back in the box and replaced the lid.

"This box says 1945," said Jaime as she took the lid off. She pulled out a large scrapbook and opened it. "Look at all these newspaper articles. They're all from the Second World War."

"My great-grandpa was in that! Let's see!" said Matt. Jaime handed him the scrapbook.

"Let's look for a box that says — what was that date? The year that Stanley Fulton disappeared?" asked Jaime.

"1937," answered Matt. He closed the scrapbook and placed it back in the box.

"Look for one that says 1937," said Jaime.

Matt wandered over to another stack of boxes and examined their labels. "Here it is," he announced. "On the bottom. It's a trunk."

"Let's get these other boxes off," said Jaime as she began pulling on the top one. "Give me a hand. This is heavy."

Matt grabbed the other end of the box. One by one, they lifted the boxes down until a large trunk labelled 1937 sat in front of them.

"Do you want to open it?" Matt asked Jaime.

"Only if you help me," she answered. Gently the two of them placed their hands on the lid.

"Ready?" asked Matt.

"I'm ready," answered Jaime. "Wait . . . "

"What now?" asked Matt.

"What if there's something icky in there?" she asked.

"Icky?" asked Matt.

"Yeah, icky. Like spiders or something."

Matt rolled his eyes. "It's not going to be full of spiders," he sighed.

"How do you know?" asked Jaime as she backed away.

"Well, I don't know. But we haven't found any spiders yet, have we?" Matt reasoned.

Jaime shook her head.

"Well, come on then. We'll open this up, and we'll find out that there is nothing unusual about it. Then you'll realize that all we saw yesterday was somebody up here doing something. Then we'll be able to get back to normal. Okay?"

Jaime looked at the trunk. "Okay."

"We'll do it together. On three. Are you ready now?" Matt asked.

Jaime spit onto her hands and rubbed them together.

"What did you do that for?" asked Matt. "That's gross."

"It's for luck," replied Jaime as she placed her hands back on the lid. "I saw it in a movie once."

"One, two . . . " Matt began.

"No spiders?" asked Jaime.

Matt groaned. "No spiders," he assured her. "One, two . . . " Matt glanced at Jaime. "Three!" he said.

Just then, the bell sounded.

Jaime and Matt stared at each other.

"Now what?" asked Jaime.

"We can't stay," answered Matt. "Not after yesterday."

Jaime quickly nodded her head. "I don't want garbage detail again."

"Let's go," urged Matt. "We'll come back at lunch."

"Okay," agreed Jaime. She patted the lid.

Matt was already heading for the door. "Come on!" he said.

"I'm coming," answered Jaime. Matt was halfway down the stairs when Jaime closed and locked the door. "We'll be back," she whispered as she placed the key in her pocket. "Don't worry, Stanley Fulton — we'll be back!"

Chapter 7

Inside the Trunk

Jaime and Matt managed to stay out of trouble all morning. As the lunch bell sounded, Mrs. Rupert approached Jaime's desk.

"Things are going much better today," Mrs. Rupert said. Jaime nodded in agreement. "It's very good to see. Off you go for lunch now."

Jaime picked up her hot lunch from the lunchroom and then she and Matt headed to the attic.

"Is that taco salad?" asked Matt.

Jaime placed the tray on the top step and reached into her pocket for the key. "Looks like it."

"Trade?" asked Matt, holding out his lunch-bag.

"You can have some of the chips," Jaime answered as the door clicked open. She glanced down the stairway and then grabbed her lunch tray. "Come on!"

Matt placed his lunch bag on the floor beside the 1937 trunk. "Okay, let's see what's in here," he said as he lifted the lid.

"Well, what's in it?" Jaime asked between sneezes. She waved at the dust flying through the air.

Matt rummaged through the trunk. "Looks like some papers. An old textbook. A shoe."

"A shoe?" asked Jaime. "Just one?"

"Yeah, just one old shoe." Matt pulled out something else. "This looks like some kind of pen," he said.

"It's a fountain pen. My grandpa has one,"

said Jamie. "What else?"

Matt pulled out some pictures of dinosaurs. "Remember? Mr. Douglas said that Stanley Fulton was fascinated by dinosaurs. Look," he said as he reached into the trunk. "It's a notebook."

"What's inside?" Jaime asked eagerly.

Matt opened the old book. "It's all about dinosaurs. It's hard to read the writing. Look. Does this say 'Iguanodon'?" Matt showed the book to Jaime.

Jaime pushed her glasses farther up her nose and leaned over to get a closer look. She nodded her head. "I think so."

Matt flipped through the book. "Look at all these pictures someone drew. I think it says 'Iguanodon' under each one."

Jaime looked at the pictures. "Iguanodons didn't look like that," she said as she shook her head. "Remember? We studied all those dinosaurs last year in Ms Reay's class."

Matt scratched his forehead. "Maybe whoever drew these wasn't a very good artist."

Matt thumbed through the book. "It says Stanley Fulton's name on the first page. It must have been his book. Maybe he didn't really know what an Iguanodon looked like." He leaned into the trunk. "There's something else in here!" he said as he pulled out a roll of paper.

"It's yellow," remarked Jaime.

"It's old, that's why," said Matt. He unrolled the large piece of yellow paper and laid it flat on the floor. "It's some kind of map," he announced.

Jaime leaned over again. "What's it a map of?"

"Just a second," said Matt. He studied the paper. "I think it's a map of the schoolyard."

"The schoolyard?" Jaime peered over his shoulder. "But that building doesn't look like our school."

Matt thought for a moment. "This is an old map," he replied. "It's from 1937. Remember? The new part of the school hadn't been built yet. This is just the original school building."

"Oh, yeah. What does it say on the bottom?" Jaime asked.

"It's hard to make out. I think it says 'Class Project.' "

"Oh," said Jaime. "Class project? About what? Hey! That looks like an X." Jaime pointed. "You know what that means!"

Matt traced his finger along a line drawn from the school to the X-mark. "It says twenty-five paces."

Jaime squealed in excitement. "Maybe there's a dinosaur buried in the field!" she shouted.

Matt gave her a doubtful look. "I don't think so," he said, "but this could be some kind of treasure map."

"Wow!" exclaimed Jaime. "And you said we wouldn't find anything unusual. Do you believe me now?"

"Well, I've got to admit that we've definitely found something interesting," said Matt as he continued to examine the map. "I love this kind of stuff."

"This must be the secret the ghost is guarding!" Jaime said excitedly. She glanced cautiously around the attic. "I wonder where the ghost is . . . "

Matt opened up his lunch bag and pulled out a sandwich. "I wonder what's buried out there."

"Matt! Don't spill anything on the map! Come on! Let's go see where it leads."

Matt swallowed his bite of sandwich and turned to face Jaime. "We'd have to dig a hole in the middle of the back field. Without anyone noticing! How do we do that?"

Jaime handed Matt some of her taco chips. "It won't be easy, I'll give you that. There must be a way, though."

"Wait, don't tell me — you'll think of something, right?"

Jaime smiled. "You know me, Matt. Of course I'll think of something."

Matt carefully rolled up the map. "Okay. Let's go outside and pace it off. At least we can see where it leads."

Jaime placed the lid back on the trunk. "We've got some time before lunch is over. Come on!" She raced to the door.

As they stood on the bottom step outside the school, Matt carefully unrolled the map and turned it around. "We're standing here, the back steps of the old part of the school." He pointed to a spot on the map. "The line on the map goes straight over there." He pointed in the direction of the playground.

Jaime glanced across a crowd of students. "Let's pace it off and see where we end up," she said. Matt nodded. "Should I take big steps or little ones?" she asked as she and Matt made their way to the bottom step.

"Let's just take normal steps. You go first. I'll follow you and we'll see if we end in the same spot."

"Okay."

Jaime began walking across the field. "One, two, three, four — " She stopped as a little boy ran in front of her. She turned to Matt. "Was I at four or five?" she asked him.

Matt shook his head. "You're *on* five."

"Oh, okay!" Jaime continued to pace and count.

"Twenty-three, twenty-four — " She carefully stepped over a small girl.

"Hey! Watch it!" said the girl.

"Twenty-five! *Twenty-five!*" Jaime yelled across the field to Matt.

Matt began pacing. When he had finished they were standing side by side.

"Matt," Jaime said as she looked down. "We're standing in the sandbox."

Chapter 8

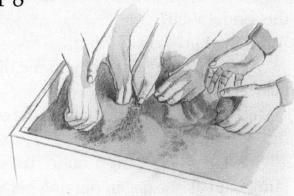

Devyn

"You mean to tell me that whatever we're looking for is buried in this sandbox?" Matt asked.

"Why not? It's a perfect place to bury something," Jaime answered.

"And this sandbox has been here since 1937?" Matt questioned.

"My dad says that he used to play in it when he was little. That's a long time ago." Jaime blew the bangs from her forehead and knelt in the sand. "Well?"

"Well what?" asked Matt.

"Well, are you going to help me dig?" Jaime answered.

Matt looked around. "Jaime, the sandbox is full of little kids."

"So? They won't even notice us, come on!" Jaime said as she began digging her hands into the cool sand.

Matt knelt beside her. "Maybe we should wait until everyone's gone."

Jaime looked at her friend. "I think Mrs. Rupert will notice if we're not in class, don't you?"

"Hey!" came a small voice. "What are you guys doing?"

Matt and Jaime looked up to see a small girl staring at them. She held a dump truck in her hands.

"We're just digging," answered Jaime.

"How come?" asked the girl.

"What's your name?" Matt asked the girl.

"Devyn," she answered.

"Well, Devyn — " Jaime started.

"Are you digging to China?" Devyn asked.

Jaime smiled at Matt and nodded. "That's right, we're digging to China."

"Hey!" Devyn yelled to her friend at the other end of the sandbox. "These big kids are digging to China!"

Another little kid stood beside Matt and Jaime. Then another one. "Can we help you dig?" asked a boy.

Jaime shrugged. "Why not?" she said. "The more people digging, the faster we'll get to China!"

The sandbox flew into a flurry of activity. Little kids were digging holes everywhere. Matt and Jaime continued to dig in the spot they had paced off.

"What are you doing?" asked the schoolyard supervisor.

"Oh hi, Mrs. Goodfellow," answered Jaime.

"We're all digging to China!" Devyn announced.

"Well, it's nice to see you all playing so nicely together," Mrs. Goodfellow said.

Matt and Jaime dug holes in the sandbox for the rest of the lunch hour. "I don't see anything," said Matt as he sat up and stretched his back. "We're just making a big mess. I'm beginning to think we're in the wrong spot. Or that there's nothing here at all."

"You'd make a lousy pirate," said Jaime as she wiped her forehead. "Pirates don't give up so easily."

"I'm not trying to be a pirate," said Matt as he flopped backward onto the sand. "How far down does this sandbox go anyway?"

"It's the deepest one I've ever seen, that's for sure!" answered Jaime as she began to dig again.

"I'll be the lookout," Matt suggested as he rolled onto his stomach.

Devyn looked up from her spot a metre away. "Did you find China yet?" she asked.

"No, Devyn, we haven't found China yet," Matt answered.

"Should we keep digging? My hole is really deep!"

"Sure, Devyn, keep digging!"

The bell sounded. "Rats!" exclaimed Jaime. "I'll bet we're really close. Probably just a little farther. We'll have to finish during afternoon recess."

Matt stood up and brushed the sand off his jeans. He looked at all the holes in the sand. "Look how many kids were digging!"

"Can we play with you again at recess?" Devyn said as she wiped her hands on her sleeves. "It's fun."

"Sure, Devyn," Jaime answered.

That afternoon, quiet reading dragged on as Jaime kept looking from her magazine to the clock. She shifted in her chair and let out a sigh.

"Jaime? Is anything wrong?" Mrs. Rupert asked from behind her desk.

"No. Is it almost time for gym?"

"No," Mrs. Rupert answered. "We still have another fifteen minutes."

"Oh." Jaime let out another sigh and continued flipping pages.

There was a knock on the door and Jaime looked up to see Mr. Turkle standing in the doorway. "Excuse me for a minute," said Mrs. Rupert as she walked into the hallway. Jaime turned around and looked across the room at Matt. He was peering over his book toward the doorway.

"I see," Jaime heard Mrs. Rupert say. "Thank you, Mr. Turkle." She walked back into the classroom and stood at the front of the room. "I have to interrupt your reading for just a minute, class," she said. "Mr. Turkle is going around to every classroom to see who knows about some students being up in the attic at lunch time."

She scanned the classroom for an instant and locked eyes with Jaime. Jaime quickly looked down at her magazine, then shot a quick glance toward Matt, who was digging around in his desk. "Apparently, whoever it was left their lunches up there, a tray and a bag lunch."

Jaime pulled her magazine closer. Mrs. Rupert went on. "Well, if you know anything about it, please let me know. The attic is out of bounds to all students. You can go back to reading now for a few minutes." Jaime was sure that Mrs. Rupert was staring right at her. She was careful not to look up.

On the way into the gym, Matt pulled on Jaime's sleeve and let the gym door close in front of them. "She knows it was us! She was looking right at me!" Matt blurted out.

"And me!" Jamie agreed.

"We have to tell them it was us. I have a feeling that they're going to find out anyway." Matt sounded desperate.

"Then we'll never solve this mystery, Matt. Come on! Just a little longer. We're going to find the treasure at recess, I just know it!"

After gym it was recess again. Jaime and Matt ran outside. Devyn was already digging.

"Found anything?" Matt asked.

"Yes!" shouted Devyn as she stood up.

"What? What is it?" Jaime asked her.

Devyn grinned. "I found an old marble," she answered as she held out her palm for them to see.

"Oh . . . that's great," Jaime said.

They continued to dig throughout recess. As the bell sounded Matt stood up and rubbed the sand off his hands. "I really don't think there is anything there, Jaime. It couldn't have been buried that far down."

Jaime stood up. "I don't know, Matt. We paced it off together. We both arrived at the same spot. It has to be here somewhere."

"Can we play again tomorrow?" asked Devyn.

"Sure Devyn," answered Matt. "Come on, Jaime. We'd better get to class."

"I know," Jaime said. "But let's not give up yet."

Time passed quickly as they worked on their science projects, and at last the day was done. As Jaime and Matt opened the door after school, Devyn was waiting at the bottom of the steps for them.

"Do they have tins in China?" she asked them.

"Do they what?" Matt asked.

"Do they have tins?" Devyn asked again. "We got to play outside after recess. I was digging again, and I found this." From behind her back she pulled out an old metal box.

"Oh my gosh!" exclaimed Jaime as she reached for it. "You found it!"

"I can't believe it!" Matt said as his eyes widened. "There really was treasure down there!"

"Treasure?" said Devyn. She pulled back the tin and hugged it to her chest.

"No, no. Not treasure," Matt said quickly. "We were just looking for something and you found it!"

"You said you were digging to China," Devyn said. She frowned.

"We're sorry," Jaime said. "Digging was more fun that way. But I'll tell you what. You let Matt and I have the box and we promise to tell you everything that's in it tomorrow."

"You're just saying that," Devyn said as

she hugged the tin even tighter. "Big kids always say that."

"We promise. We'll even pinky-swear," Jaime said.

"Pinky-swear?" Devyn seemed interested.

"Pinky-swear," Jaime said again as she held out the little finger on her right hand. "We promise to play with you again tomorrow."

"Will you pinky-swear too?" Devyn looked at Matt.

"Sure." Matt held out a little finger. "I'll pinky-swear too."

They all shook their little fingers together and Devyn handed Jaime the tin.

"Thanks, Devyn," Jaime said. "We'll see you tomorrow." Devyn turned and walked away. Jaime turned to Matt. "We really have something! Where do you want to open it? I don't want to open it here. Everyone will see."

"Yes," Matt agreed.

Jaime looked at her watch. "I don't have much time either," she said excitedly. "After all the trouble I've been in lately, my mom and dad want me home right after school." She jumped up and down with excitement.

Matt grabbed her elbows until she stopped jumping. They stared at each other. "The treehouse!" they said together.

Chapter 9

The Tin Box

Matt and Jamie dropped their bikes in Matt's yard. Quickly, they climbed the treehouse ladder. Then Matt pulled it up, and Jamie closed the treehouse door.

Matt sat down on a wooden crate as Jaime fumbled to open her backpack.

"Hurry up!" urged Matt.

"I'm trying!" Jaime said as she struggled with the knot. Finally it was open. Carefully she pulled the tin out and laid it down on the floor.

Jaime and Matt stared at the small tin box.

"What do you think is in there?" asked Matt.

"I don't know," answered Jaime. "Who's going to open it?"

"It was your idea about this ghost thing," answered Matt. He pushed the tin toward Jaime. "You open it."

"Me?" asked Jaime. "Are you sure?"

"Yeah. Hurry up, before Zoe gets home," Matt urged. "Let's see what's inside."

Jaime pulled the tin toward her. She carefully wiped the sand off it. "Ready?" she asked.

"Yeah, yeah, I'm ready. Hurry up!" Matt said.

Gently Jaime reached for the top of the box. She pulled on it. "It's stuck," she said.

"Yank on it," said Matt. "Just pull off the lid!"

Jaime grabbed the box and tugged. "It's still stuck," she said.

"Come on, Jaime," urged Matt. "You can do it!"

Jaime dug in with her fingernails and pulled. The lid popped off the box and flew through the air. "It's off," she said.

"What's inside?" asked Matt. "What is it?"

Jaime pulled out a piece of paper. "A newspaper clipping."

"What does it say?" asked Matt. "Let me see!"

Jaime read the headline. "King George VI was crowned on May 12th," she said.

"King who?" asked Matt. "What else is in there?"

Jaime pulled out another piece of paper. "Somebody named Joe Louis won a fight," she said.

"What else?" asked Matt.

Jaime pulled out more pieces of paper. "The Red Wings won the Stanley Cup. Hey — here's a story about Babe Ruth."

"Keeping looking," said Matt. "There's got to be something really interesting in there!"

Jaime rummaged carefully through the box. "Another newspaper clipping," she said. "This is about the *Hindenburg*."

"Oh my gosh, was Stanley Fulton on the *Hindenburg*?" asked Matt. "Is that why he disappeared?"

Jaime checked the date on the newspaper. "Couldn't have been," she answered. "It went down in May. Remember? Mr. Douglas said Stanley Fulton was here until the end of the school year."

"Oh yeah," remembered Matt. "Maybe he was on the *Titanic!* Maybe that's why he never came back."

Jaime stopped for a minute and scratched her chin. "I don't know when that was. Maybe there's something in here about that . . . "

Matt glanced over the articles lying on the floor. "This looks like a time capsule. You know, where people put a whole bunch of stuff into a box and then bury it."

Jaime stared at Matt. "Why do they do that?" she asked.

Matt shrugged. "Maybe it's so that the people who find it will know what life was like a long time ago. My great-grandpa told me once about a time capsule he buried. But he can't remember where he buried it."

"There's something else in here," Jaime said as she reached into the box. She pulled out one last newspaper clipping and studied it. "'Tallest dinosaur,'" she read.

"Tallest dinosaur?" Matt asked.

"Yeah. It says here that Dr. Brown found the first bones of an actual Iguanodon," Jaime said.

"Iguanodon?" Matt said. "That's not the tallest dinosaur, is it? What else does it say?"

"It says," continued Jaime, "the site is in . . . the paper is torn and I can't read the name of the place. Anyway, it says that excavation is under way. They're using steam shovels."

"What's the date on the paper?" asked Matt.

Jaime looked at the top of the clipping. "All it says is June. The date was ripped off."

"What's circled?" asked Matt. "There's something circled in pen there." There was a small map printed with the story.

"The name of a town in Wyoming is circled. That's somewhere in the United States, isn't it?" Jaime asked.

"I don't know. I think so," said Matt.

Jaime squinted at the map. Then she sat up and handed it to Matt. "It's Rock Springs," she said. "That's what Stanley Fulton was talking about just before he disappeared!"

"Rock Springs is a place?" asked Matt.

"It looks like it." Matt read the entire article aloud. When he was done, he was silent for a moment. Then he said, "I wonder. . . . What if Stanley Fulton read this, got really excited, and went to Rock Springs to join the excavation?"

"Yeah," agreed Jaime, "and then he stayed there, to help dig up other dinosaur bones."

"So, that's why he never came back?" wondered Matt.

Jaime rolled onto her back on the treehouse

floor. "Digging up dinosaurs seems a lot more exciting than being a school principal. Would you come back?"

Matt shook his head. "Not a chance."

Jaime sat up quickly. "That still doesn't explain the ghost!"

"Hey, Matt!" came a voice from below. "Are you up in your dollhouse again?"

Matt rolled his eyes. "Zoe."

"You have to unload the dishwasher. It's your turn!" Zoe called.

"I'll be down in a second," Matt answered.

"I'm not doing it for you!" Zoe yelled.

"I said I'd be down in a second!" Matt called again.

Jaime gathered all of the articles and placed them back into the box. "I'll look through this stuff again tonight," she said as she put the box into her backpack. "We'll figure out where the ghost comes in."

Matt opened the treehouse door and put the ladder down. "Okay."

Jaime climbed down and mounted her bike.

"There must be something else in here. Something we've missed."

"Call me," Matt shouted as she pedalled away.

Chapter 10

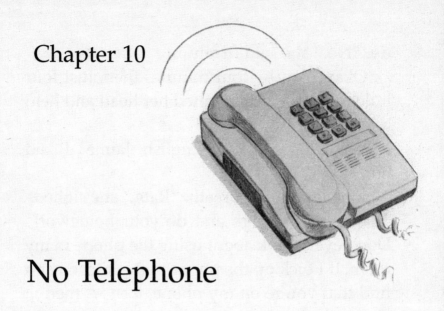

No Telephone

"Please, Mom. Just one phone call!" Jaime pleaded.

Mrs. Forrester looked up from the newspaper. "Not a chance," she replied. "Don't bother arguing about it either. It's your own fault."

"But, Mom, just a quick call!" Jaime begged. "Five minutes!"

Mrs. Forrester folded the paper and stood

up. "No," she said firmly.

"Okay, okay — four minutes then. Just four little minutes?" Jaime tilted her head and held her breath.

"Am I not speaking English, Jaime? I said no."

Jaime let out her breath. "Rats," she sighed.

"Now, off you go and do your homework. Don't even think about using the phone in my room. If I pick up the phone in the kitchen and find that you're on my phone, then ... then ... you won't be able to use the phone for the rest of your life."

Jaime grabbed the bannister and pulled herself up the stairs. She hesitated at the entrance to her parents' room, then hurried on. In her own room, she laid her backpack on the floor and pulled out the small tin box.

She read the articles inside it again. "Would Stanley Fulton really leave everything behind and go to Rock Springs?" she wondered aloud.

After supper Jaime searched her CD

encyclopedia for more information. Sure enough, it said that the first bones from a real Iguanodon were discovered in Rock Springs, Wyoming. Then she checked out information on *Titanic*, just in case.

"April 15, 1912," she sighed. "Way too early."

The phone rang and Jaime leapt up to answer it.

"Sit down, young lady," said her mother. "No phone means that you can't talk to anyone, even if they call you." Mrs. Forrester rounded the corner to the kitchen.

"Sorry, Matt," Jaime heard her mother say. "Jaime can't use the phone for a while. Okay, I'll give her the message." Jaime's mother hung up the phone.

"What did he say?" Jaime asked.

"Are you two working on an extra project at school or something?" Mrs. Forrester asked her.

"Kind of, yeah," Jaime answered. "It's a history thing."

"Oh. Well, Matt says he'll meet you at school early. Now it's time to shut that down and get ready for bed. Homework all done?"

"I think so," Jaime answered.

"Okay, then, off you go."

In the morning, Jaime sat at the kitchen table with her dad.

"Everything going okay at school, kiddo?" he asked.

Jaime blew on her porridge. "Yes, Dad, everything's okay." She swallowed a spoonful. "Yow! This porridge sure is hot!"

"Are you in a hurry this morning? You're trying to eat it too fast," Mr. Forrester said.

"I have to meet Matt," Jaime answered.

"Are you keeping out of trouble these days?" Jaime's dad asked her.

"Yup. I haven't been in trouble at school for a day or so now." Jaime cleaned out her bowl and placed it in the sink.

"Keep working at it, Jaime," Mr. Forrester said as he leaned over and kissed the top of her head.

"Yeah, Dad. I will. See you later," Jaime said as she raced up the stairs to her room.

When she was dressed, she put the tin box into her backpack and ran downstairs again, grabbing a recess snack from the fridge as she passed through the kitchen. "Bye, Mom!" she called as she headed out the back door.

Jaime grabbed her bike and pedalled to the usual spot at the end of the street to wait for Matt. Finally, she saw him coming toward her.

"Man!" Matt said as he skidded to a stop. "I tried to call you last night."

"I know," Jaime replied. "Not using the phone is torture."

"What about me?" Matt said. "I couldn't talk to you on the phone *and* I couldn't watch TV. I can't wait until this week is over."

"Yeah," agreed Jaime. "Me too."

"Jaime, I had the weirdest dream last night. Promise you won't laugh?"

"I promise," Jaime answered. "What was it about?"

"It was about Stanley Fulton. He came into my room and said he wasn't going to leave until we had found something in the box. I woke up and couldn't get back to sleep for a long time."

Jaime's eyes widened. "Maybe he was trying to tell you something!"

"It was freaky, Jaime." Matt wiped his arm across his forehead. "Did you find anything else in that box?"

Jaime began pedalling. "No. I did find out that Stanley Fulton couldn't have been on the *Titanic*. That was a really long time ago."

"Oh," said Matt, catching up to his friend.

"So," said Jaime, "are you thinking what I'm thinking?"

"That depends," Matt replied. "What are you thinking?" He pulled ahead of Jaime.

"I was thinking . . . " Jaime answered, pedalling faster, ". . . that we need to get back up into the attic this morning."

Matt began to pick up speed. He passed Jaime again. "I was thinking the same thing,"

he smiled as he raced Jaime to the school. "I think I need to take another look in that trunk!"

Chapter 11

Once More Into the Attic

Matt and Jaime wheeled into the parking lot and locked their bikes in the bike rack.

"You've still got the key, right?" Matt asked.

Jaime patted the pocket of her vest. "Right here," she answered.

Matt opened the door of the school and the two of them stepped slowly inside. The door shut loudly behind them.

"I thought you had the door," Jaime whispered.

"I thought *you* had it," Matt whispered back.

"Come on," Jaime said as she headed up the attic stairs. She dug into her pocket and pulled out the key.

"We've got to give that back," Matt said.

"We will," answered Jaime, "as soon as we find out who was in the attic."

The door clicked and Matt pushed it open. "Here we are again," he said.

Jaime looked around. "Why would Stanley Fulton's ghost hang around here?" she asked.

"I think the answer must be in this trunk," Matt said as he threw down his backpack and lifted the lid. "Hey — " Matt stopped. "We don't even know if Stanley Fulton is dead, let alone a ghost."

"Matt," Jaime gave him a strange look. "If he became principal in 1914, he'd be way over a hundred years old now."

"So he's probably not alive?" asked Matt.

"I can pretty well guarantee it. Come on, let's go through this stuff again."

Matt reached for the notebook. "Maybe he's

looking for this," he said.

"What do you mean? Why the notebook?" asked Jaime.

Matt gently began thumbing through the pages. "These pictures of Iguanodons . . . " he said. "Maybe he found out that they were all wrong."

"Hmm . . . " said Jaime. "I think I'm beginning to see." She thought a while. Then she said, "Before the discovery at Rock Springs, people didn't truly know what this dinosaur looked like. They probably only had a few fossils and footprints here and there. Stanley Fulton put them together, like a puzzle, and made these sketches of what he thought the Iguanodon could have looked like." Jaime stopped to catch her breath.

"But then the bones were found," Matt continued, "and everyone knew what an Iguanodon really looked like."

Jamie nodded. "So maybe he wanted to come back and fix his sketches," she concluded. She looked around the attic. "Mr.

Fulton?" she whispered. "Mr. Fulton, are you there?"

"Are you crazy?" asked Matt.

"Shh! Just be quiet," Jaime said. "Mr. Fulton? If you're here, we just want you to know that it's okay. Everybody knows what an Iguanodon looks like now, so you don't have to fix your drawings. "

Jaime looked at Matt. Matt looked at Jaime. She said, "Mr. Fulton? Maybe if you could just give us a sign or something. Just to show you understand — "

"Hey!" boomed a voice from behind them.

Jaime and Matt shrieked. Then they slowly turned around. "M–Mr. F–Fulton?" Jaime's voice shook.

A tall figure was standing in the doorway. "Who?" he asked.

Jamie stared. "Are you Mr. Fulton?" she asked.

Matt blinked twice and then rubbed his eyes. "You're not see-through or anything," he said in a very quiet voice.

The tall figure began walking toward them. "What are you two talking about?" it asked.

"Mr. Turkle!" Jaime and Matt scrambled against the trunk.

"We . . . we . . . we . . . " Jaime stammered.

Mr. Turkle stopped. "What are you doing up here? How did you get in? Were you up here yesterday?"

Jaime closed the trunk and stood up. "What are we doing up here? That's a very good question, Mr. Turkle. We were trying to . . . we were trying to . . . "

"We were trying to solve another mystery," Matt said.

"A mystery?" asked Mr. Turkle. He frowned at them. Then his face softened a little. "Well, I guess an attic is as good a place as any for a mystery." He pulled a large picture frame off one of the shelves and leaned it against the wall. "What kind of mystery?"

"The mystery of Stanley Fulton," said Jaime as she watched Mr. Turkle pull another frame off the shelf and lean it against the first one.

"Stanley Fulton? You mean this guy?" asked Mr. Turkle as he pulled another frame off the shelf and turned it around. "The guy in this picture?"

Jaime jumped back in surprise. "That's him," she answered.

Matt opened the 1937 trunk again. "We found some interesting stuff in here."

"Those boxes are full of interesting artifacts," Mr. Turkle said. "Now, about you two being in the attic . . . "

"Wait a second, Jaime," said Matt as he flipped a book over. "This is stuck to the bottom," he said. He carefully pulled off a newspaper article. "Oh my gosh!" he exclaimed.

"What?" asked Jaime. "What have you found?"

"Look at this picture." Matt held out the article. "Who is that?"

Jaime pushed her glasses up her nose and peered. "It looks like — "

"Stanley Fulton. In September of 1937." Matt

quickly read through the article. "It says that he went down to Rock Springs to visit his son."

"So?" asked Jaime. "What else does it say?"

"It says that he was offered a job at a school down there. It says he won't be returning to Fulton Street School."

"Is that all?" Jamie was disappointed. "There's nothing about dinosaurs in that story."

"Yes, there is," said Mr. Turkle. Jamie and Matt looked at him in surprise.

"Stanley Fulton's son was a paleontologist," Mr. Turkle continued. "He was working on an important discovery down there."

"That's why Mr. Fulton was so interested in dinosaurs," Matt said. "His son was a dinosaur digger."

Jaime closed the lid of the trunk. "That still doesn't explain the face in the window."

"Hey," Matt said as he pointed to the shelves, "why are all those pictures here?"

"They had pictures taken every year.

There's a whole bunch here of old Stanley."
Mr. Turkle put the picture he was holding on
the window sill. "I'm moving them downstairs to the basement. Mr. Douglas wants new
shelves put up. These ones are old and falling
apart."

Matt stared at the picture on the window sill.
Then he looked at Jaime.

"Were you here on Monday morning?" Matt
asked Mr. Turkle.

"Monday? Yeah, I come up here every
chance I get, trying to get these pictures
moved."

"Do you always lean a picture against the
window like that?" Matt asked. "With the face
looking out?"

Mr. Turkle shrugged. "Some of them. It
depends. Why?"

Matt looked at Jaime again. She shrugged
sheepishly at him.

"I sort them by size. Makes them easier to
carry. I take one load down and then come up
for the next," Mr. Turkle explained.

"And then you sort some more?" asked Matt.

"If I have time," answered Mr. Turkle. "What's all this about?"

Matt took a deep breath. "Then on Monday, you could have taken a load down to the basement, and fifteen or so minutes later, you could have rested another picture right there?" Matt pointed toward the window.

"Yeah, I guess." Mr. Turkle took off his cap and scratched the top of his head. "You're asking some weird questions, kid."

"I think we just figured everything out. Thanks for your help, Mr. Turkle," Matt said as the bell sounded. "Come on, let's go," he said to Jaime.

"Wait a second, you two. You still haven't told me how you got in here. But I think I know." Mr. Turkle stopped them as they headed toward the door. He held out his hand.

Jaime pulled the attic key out of her pocket and gave it to Mr. Turkle. "We kind of borrowed it. Just for a little while."

Mr. Turkle shook his head. "You two have got to learn how to stay out of trouble. You're lucky that nobody noticed this was missing."

"I know," Jaime said.

"You'd better go before you're late for class," Mr. Turkle shook his head. "Kids," he muttered.

"Jaime," said Matt as they started down the stairwell, "I don't know how I ever let you talk me into these — "

"I know, I know. Don't be mad, Matt. You were pretty convinced there was a ghost up there, too, you know."

Matt waved his hands in the air. "I am the ghost of Stanley Fulton," he droned, "I'm here to find my notebook!"

"No," Jaime said, as she waved her hands in the air, "I'm here because I lost my shoe and I think I left it in one of those trunks!" They burst out laughing.

"Where's my treasure?" asked a little voice.

Jamie looked down. "Hi, Devyn," she said.

"There wasn't any treasure. Just a bunch of newspaper articles."

"Really?" asked Devyn.

"Honest," Jaime replied. "There was no treasure."

"Okay," smiled Devyn. "Remember? You said you'd play with me today."

"Oh yeah," said Matt. "Well, we'll see you on the playground, okay, Devyn?"

"Okay!" Devyn answered. She turned and walked toward her classroom.

Jaime and Matt sat down on the bottom step. "We do have to play with her," Matt said. "We promised."

"I know," Jaime sighed. "We pinky-swore."

"What do little kids play anyway?" asked Matt.

"I don't know," Jaime answered. "I have a cousin that's little. She has a really good imagination. She likes to pretend stuff."

"Oh," said Matt.

"Excuse me," said Mr. Turkle as he walked down the stairs with an armload of pictures.

Matt and Jaime moved aside and then back again. Matt nudged his friend. "Like pretending there are aliens in the basement? Or pretending there's a ghost in the attic?"

Jaime shot Matt a quick glance. "It's not the same," she said.

"I see," Matt said. "Whatever you say. Hey!" He stood up quickly. "We'd better get to class before — "

"Would Matt Dias and Jaime Forrester please report to the office," came a voice over the loudspeaker.

Jaime groaned. "We're late again!"

"Straight to the office this time." Matt's eyes grew wide. "We're really in for it this time."

Jaime stood up. "It's almost spring break. What can happen in three days?"

"Knowing you, Jaime," said Matt, "almost *anything*."

Suzan Reid has always loved writing. When she was little, she used to write stories for her dad and tuck them into his lunch bag so he wouldn't be lonely at work. Now she has written three picture books — *Grandpa Dan's Toboggan Ride, Follow That Bus!* and *The Meat Eaters Arrive* — and one other Shooting Star book, *Aliens in the Basement*.

A full-time teacher, Suzan loves music, sports and swimming in her backyard pool. She lives in Westbank, British Columbia, with her husband, two daughters, a turtle and a very large dog.

Have you read these Shooting Star books?

❏ *Aliens in the Basement* • Suzan Reid

❏ *The Big Race!* • Sylvia McNicoll

❏ *A Ghost in the Attic* • Suzan Reid

❏ *Liar, Liar, Pants on Fire* • Gordon Korman

❏ *The Lost Locket* • Carol Matas

❏ *Monsters in the School* • Martyn Godfrey

❏ *Princesses Don't Wear Jeans* • Brenda Bellingham

❏ *Project Disaster* • Sylvia McNicoll

❏ *School Campout* • Becky Citra

❏ *Sleepover Zoo* • Brenda Kearns

❏ *Starring Me!* • Cathy Miyata

❏ *Wonder Dog* • Beverly Scudamore

❏ *Worm Pie* • Beverly Scudamore